I0624610

Victoria Browne

Slip

Neville House Publishing

This Book novella is entirely a work of fiction. The names, characters and incidents portrayed therein are creations of the author's imagination. Any resemblance to actual persons, living or dead, is purely coincidental.

Published by Neville House Publishing

Copyright © Victoria Browne 2017

The author's rights are fully asserted. The right of Victoria Browne to be identified as the author of this work has been asserted by her in accordance with the Copyright, Designs and Patents Act 1988.

First published by
Neville House Publishing in 2017.

A CIP Catalogue of this book is available
from the British Library

Paperback: 978-0-9928083-6-5
EBook ISBN: 978-0-9928083-7-2

All rights reserved; no part of this publication may be reproduced, stored in a retrieval system, or transmitted, in any form or by any means, electronic, mechanical, photocopying, recording or otherwise, without the prior written permission of the publisher. Nor be circulated in any form of binding or cover other than that in which it is published and a similar condition including this condition being imposed on the subsequent purchaser.

Printed and distributed by
Kindle Direct Publishing

BY THE SAME AUTHOR

Gut Feeling
The Honey Trap
Notting Hill Gossip

To My Mother

Slip

The door to the nursing home swung open faster than Emily had estimated, slamming into the already paint-chipped wall. She rushed through the door, passing an old lady mopping the floor.

"Slowly, dear, you'll slip," a frail voice said.

Emily heard the warning too late and felt her feet slip from under her.

The old woman approached, holding out a hand, and helped Emily to her feet again. "I did tell you to slow down," she said.

"Yes, yes, you did. Thanks," Emily said. She let go of the lady's hand and smoothed down her suit jacket.

"Are you hurt?" the old lady asked.

"Um . . . no—no." For a split second, Emily forgot what she was doing there. Was it for work? She blinked rapidly. Or to visit someone? Yes—to visit, although she struggled to remember who. "Er, I'm here to see . . ." *Why can't I remember?* And then, as if someone had answered the question in her mind, she knew. "Abigail," she said triumphantly. "Abigail Neville. Can you tell me what room she's in?" She rubbed the back of her head.

Emily watched as the tiny lines that traced the old lady's face deepened. She wasn't sure if the woman's expression was of concern or perhaps trapped wind. After all, she looked very old.

"Is your head OK, my dear?" the woman asked. "Did you hit it when you slipped? I'm a first-aider; I can take a look. Here, sit." She pointed to a bench next to the reception desk.

Why do I want to see Abigail? Emily found herself thinking, ignoring the old lady's first aid offer. She squeezed her eyes tight, then opened them with new clarity. She wanted to know why Abigail had kept it all a secret.

"No. Thanks—I'm fine, really," Emily insisted. "So, Abigail Neville—what room, please?"

A delightful smile replaced the woman's concern. "Are you her daughter?"

"Um, no, I'm her—" She stopped. She could have sworn the old lady had just twitched, like a glitch in her vision. Emily squeezed her eyes shut again and reopened them. Maybe she *had* hit her head.

Emily noticed the old lady angling her ear toward her as if to hear better. "She's just moved here from Sun Life," Emily continued, "and I—"

"Who, dear? Abigail?"

Emily's phone vibrated, indicating yet another work email. It was Mark, her boss. He wanted to know if she had won the contract or not. She swiped her finger across the screen before answering the woman. "Yes!" Emily said, typing a short reply back to Mark.

I'M HERE NOW, TEXT YOU SOON.

She slid her phone back into her pocket and suddenly felt confused. Was she there for the contract or Abigail? The thought of work faded, and Abigail came back to the forefront of her mind.

"My dear, Abigail's been here six months now." The old woman shook her head. "She hasn't had any visitors, so she'll be pleased to see you—where's your mum?" She looked at Emily's phone, then at Emily. Her stare felt intrusive.

A sharp pain cut across Emily's eye, and she winced. "With respect, I'm not sure if that is any of your business," she said, stepping back. The woman flickered like a hologram, and Emily looked away before adjusting her sight again.

"Are you sure you're OK, dear?"

"Fine—I'm fine." She pressed her fingers hard against the side of her head. "So what room?"

"I'm Valerie." The woman chuckled and started to mop the floor again. "I used to live in Texas," she said randomly. "She never asked me to stay . . ."

Emily was growing impatient with Valerie, so she ignored the old woman's ramblings and surveyed her surroundings, looking for someone else to help her. There was a large communal area dotted with mismatching tables and hideous floral sofas, but she saw no sign of nursing home staff. She noticed a small, white-haired lady who sat gazing out of the window overlooking well-manicured gardens. The lady gave a sideways glance at Emily and waved. Emily waved back hesitantly.

"Who's the lady by the window?" Emily turned back to Valerie, who was still rambling about scarlet fever or something; Emily hadn't been listening.

"Sorry, dear, window?" Valerie craned her neck.

"Emily—my name's Emily. Who's that sitting by the wind—" Emily felt her phone vibrate in her suit pocket. "Sorry, one sec." She scrambled for her phone. "*Shit*," she mumbled under her breath, reading a text from Mark, who was now reminding her that she had forgotten to submit her month's expenses again, and he would be sending them off in an hour. "OK. Abigail—do you know where she is? I really need to get a move on."

"Yes, dear."

Emily looked at Valerie impatiently as the old lady fished around in the front pocket of her apron, eventually pulling out a large, ruby-set ring. She slid it onto her finger slowly, exacerbating Emily's frustration.

"I take it off to clean," Valerie explained.

"Right. So Abigail's room?" Emily nodded.

"Yes. Come, follow me." They moved across the communal seating area slower than Emily would have liked. As Emily followed Valerie, they passed the window where the old, white-haired lady sat. She didn't look at Emily.

"Who's that sitting there?" Emily kept her voice low.

"No . . . I don't sit there anymore, dear," Valerie replied.

Oh god, why are old people such hard work? Emily rolled her eyes to the ceiling. "No, I said who's—"

A loud smash interrupted her and echoed through the room. She looked over to see a man with a walker who had crashed into a table of cups and was fumbling to right himself.

Valerie hurried—or tried as best she could to hurry—over to the gentleman's aid, shouting over her shoulder as she went, "Fourth floor—room 111, dear."

Emily continued through the communal area, watching Valerie fussing over the elderly man, and wondered how old people managed to look after other old people safely. Surely there must be regulations about that.

Standing at the elevator, she scrolled through her emails, not really paying attention to them. Her head now throbbed. When the elevator didn't come, she jabbed her finger at the button again before hearing a ping, and the silver doors finally opened. She took the elevator to the fourth floor.

Worn blue paisley carpet stuck to her stilettos with each step. Emily made her way to the far end of the lightless corridor, eventually reaching a white door with the room number 111 and a low-set spyhole. Nausea rushed her jaw, making her mouth salivate. Her peripheral vision blurred. The door engulfed everything, and for a moment, she forgot why she was there again. Emily squeezed her eyes shut once more.

What is happening?

Opening her eyes, she raised a heavy arm to knock at the door.

Placing her house keys neatly on a hook in the kitchen, Emily dimmed the lights. She hoisted the plastic carrier bag she held up onto the countertop and retrieved a tin of chopped tomatoes and a bottle of red wine before chopping an onion. Her pan of red meat spat as she tossed in the diced vegetables.

Leaving the pan, she walked with a glass of red wine toward the living room, her stiletto heels heavy on the wood floor. She kicked off her shoes, leaving them by the front door, and nuzzled her feet into a pair of slippers before turning into the living room.

The lights were already on low, and she wondered if she had left them on this morning. Trying to remember, Emily pulled a weary hand down her face. She looked at the wine and wondered why she was drinking. She took a sip, ignoring her own thoughts.

She reached for her phone, but she was no longer wearing her suit jacket; it was hanging on the banister out in the hallway. When had she removed her jacket? She was becoming increasingly aware that her memory had gaps, but she swiftly forgot her concerns.

With careful steps, Emily walked over to the fireplace, holding out her hand to the flames.

Who lit the fire? The fleeting thought faded as quickly as it had come.

She reached for a gold-framed photo that was sitting on top of the steel mantel. Emily looked at the middle-aged woman in the photo, frozen in time. She looked so beautiful, even if she *was* imitating the oversized gorilla statue that she stood next to. Her nose was squished together, and her lips parted to show her teeth. Emily smiled.

Who took the photo? Was it me? Why couldn't she remember?

In a soft voice, Emily addressed the photo and said, "I saw her today."

Talking to a picture felt nice and not weird at all. She liked the feeling—it felt therapeutic. She took another sip of wine.

"She misses you." The photo stared back at Emily, motionless in time.

Smelling the food, Emily remembered her dinner.

Returning from the kitchen moments later, she ate perched on a footstool by the fire. She placed her glass of red wine at her feet, careful not to spill any on the white rug. The warmth of the fire felt soothing on her cheeks as she stared up at the picture on the mantel, chewing her food slowly.

"She waited for you to come for her. Why didn't you?" Emily paused, as if waiting for a reply. "She was frightened. She said she couldn't see out; she said the windows were too high." She felt odd all of a sudden, homesick, though she didn't know why. She wasn't a child, nor was she away from home. She took a mouthful of wine and continued. "But you know all that, don't you? You were scared too; you just never said anything." The fire crackled and spat, and embers fell onto the stone base.

Emily placed the unfinished food on the floor, her appetite now gone, and picked up her glass. She stood in front of the mantel, facing the photo again and looking at the woman.

"She doesn't regret moving to Texas; that was the right thing to do. No—she said she went about it the wrong way." Spontaneously, Emily felt her legs shudder as another feeling—regret—affected her, and her thoughts were momentarily disabled. Once the feeling had passed, she continued. "She felt bitter, said you waved her off at the airport and didn't even cry. But that's not the way, is it? It's not your way. You hide emotions, British stiff upper lip and all that."

Emily winced and rubbed the back of her head. She couldn't remember if she had taken a headache pill already.

She tuned back to the mantel. "The calls home became less frequent, and she stopped visiting. After all, you never visited her." Emily jumped as an ember hit her ankle. "Ouch." She brushed at her foot. A surge of electricity flickered the lights in the house.

"After Jack left, she said she should have come home, but she was young and angry, stubborn—she played the victim, somehow hoping you would call and tell her to come home. But you didn't, and she resented you for that . . . but she loved you. You were her big sister. She just wanted to hear how much you missed her and to come home. To see your emotions, cry, scream, hate—anything."

The fire was hot, and Emily took off her Trousers, throwing them over the arm of her worn brown leather sofa. She let her white shirt fall over her bottom and walked back to the steel mantel.

"She met Chuck, and things changed. She was happy—she really was. She wants you to know that. She said that it's important you know. She was truly happy. She just wishes things had been different and you could have been a part of their lives." Emily stared at the photo. "She's sorry."

Emily fell silent. She felt sad relaying the story, though not for them but for herself. She tried to think about her own life but couldn't do it. All thoughts bounced back to that morning, to Valerie and the nursing home, and then to Abigail. Abigail. The name felt different now. Did she know another Abigail?

One at the home and another? This thought sat in her mind for a while before losing its meaning. Emily's vision flickered, and the next thing she saw was the stairs she was climbing to bed.

The door to the nursing home swung open faster than Emily had estimated, slamming into the already paint-chipped wall. Emily rushed through the door, passing an old lady mopping the floor.

"Slowly, dear, you'll slip," a frail voice said.

A powerful sense of déjà vu destabilized her. *Valerie?* Emily thought of the name and slowed her pace as she made for the elevators. *Why does this all feel so familiar?* Her thoughts were momentary. A second feeling of déjà vu overwhelmed her and made her stumble slightly.

She passed a white-haired lady by the window, and for some reason, she half expected to see a man with a walker. She gave her head a small shake and felt a shooting pain dart across the top of her brow.

As she stood by the elevator, she looked back into the communal area at the mismatching furniture and the white-haired lady by the window.

She looks peaceful. She heard a ping, indicating the elevator had arrived, but kept gazing at the old lady's profile. She watched the woman turn slowly to look in Emily's direction. Her long, white hair hung down each side of her face and looked strangely spooky, yet Emily didn't feel frightened. Their eyes met, and she smiled at the lady. Emily strained to see the lady's facial characteristics, but she couldn't—or at least, she couldn't seem to hold onto them in her mind. The lady looked away.

That's freaking odd. The doors to the elevator closed. "Shit." Emily jabbed at the button. "Oh, come on."

Emily stood looking up at the floor counter above the elevator as it moved up the floors. Again, she found herself wondering what she was doing there. A smash echoed through the communal area, distracting her. She peered around the corner to see what the commotion was.

"You have to be kidding me," she said, watching Valerie help a man with a walker negotiate the tea table on the far side of the room. She wondered if there was a record for instances of déjà vu in one day, and if so, whether she was in the running to break it. Emily heard the ping of the elevator and rushed to make the doors. She took the elevator to the fourth floor, and on the way up, her thoughts turned to Valerie. She couldn't remember the last time she had been to the home, or how she knew Valerie. Was she dreaming? She immediately laughed at her thought.

The doors opened, and clarity returned—she was going to room 111. She stepped into the dark corridor for the second time. Reaching room 111, she raised her arm—it felt light, and her knock felt flimsy. Had she even knocked loudly enough? Emily rubbed her temples as her vision brightened and a haze impaired her right eye, disorientating her sight. The door opened. A brilliant light flooded Emily's sight, and then she saw Valerie gesturing for her to come inside.

What is Valerie doing here? Stepping over the threshold, Emily blinked to focus better.

"Valerie?" she said.

Confused, she swung around, trying to see through the bright light. What was going on? She reached out to find a table or bed to stabilize herself, but there was nothing there—nothing. The blood pounding in Emily's ears deafened out all sound. She couldn't see—why couldn't she see?

Panicked, she called out again, louder this time. "Valerie?"

She rubbed her eyes and then opened them wide, frantically looking around. She saw nothing but darkness.

Blinded—I'm blind? Fuck, what's going on? Terror gripped her.

She looked down at her feet and screamed. She wasn't blind, but she was frozen by fear. She stared down at her feet, scared to move, even to breathe. Below her feet was nothing. Absolutely nothing. She slowed her breath, raising her head ever so slowly.

"Valerie?" she whispered, scanning the place she was in, whatever it was—wherever it was.

Was she even alive, or was she really dreaming? Emily looked at her hands, turning her palms upward. She watched embers leaping from her palms.

She looked up to see Valerie in the distance. "Valerie!" Emily cried out. "What's happening to me, Valerie? Where am I—what is this place?"

Valerie didn't reply. Emily heard a man calling and swung her head toward where the door had been. But still she saw nothing—she floated in the middle of nothing, embers falling from her hands, watching Valerie move further away.

"Valerie. What's going on? What's happening, Valerie—where are you going?"

Emily started to feel frantic. She felt light-headed, dizzy, and nauseous. What was happening? Who was she? Her own thoughts now felt foreign. Who was Valerie?

She suddenly thought of Abigail, then of Mark and her work contract. Nothing made sense, and yet it felt as if it should. Emily felt her fear increase—nothing seemed to connect logically. Who was Valerie? And why was Abigail in a home? Instinctively, Emily started to shake her head from side to side, as if trying to wake herself from a bad dream.

"It's OK, Emily. You slipped." Valerie's voice was weak.

"What do you mean, 'slipped'?" She strained to hear.

Emily retched as she felt a strong wave of nausea.

A sharp pain shot across her eyes, and she squeezed them tight.

What did she mean, I "slipped"?

Emily's eyes opened, and she saw a man, not geriatric old, about fifty. She couldn't make out what he was saying at first. His lips moved, but the sound was muffled. She could feel the cold, hard reception floor beneath her.

"You slipped," the man was saying. "You hurried though those doors so fast, and whoosh—you slipped. But you're OK—an ambulance is on its way."

Emily tried to sit up onto her elbow.

"No, no. Stay on the floor. Here, rest your head on this." She saw him move a cushion beneath her. "You wasn't out long, but you *did* lose consciousness for a bit. Best if you stay where you are till the medics get here, OK?"

Emily nodded, lowering herself down. She wasn't in room 111; she hadn't even gotten past reception. What had happened? Was it really all a dream? Just a knock to the head? She could see the old, concerned faces of nursing home residents gathering around. *Valerie*, she remembered.

"Um—where's Valerie?" Her voice was hoarse.

"Who?" the man questioned.

"No one; it's OK." Emily said nothing more. She lay on the cold nursing home floor, thinking about her dream. It felt so real. She struggled to comprehend what was happening—had happened. Did people have dreams when they got knocked out?

They must, she concluded. Just a knock to the head, then. She relaxed; she had imagined it all.

Her phone vibrated in her suit pocket, and she reached for it awkwardly. "Excuse me," she said to the man. "Can you help me get my phone out, please?" Her grip was light, and her hands still shaky.

The man pulled the half-retrieved phone from her pocket and handed it to her. She missed the call. It had been her boss, no doubt wanting to know how the meeting had gone. She remembered why she was really at the nursing home. She was there to secure a cleaning contract—her boss would not be pleased if this slip cost them the deal.

She called the number back and listened to the dialing tone. "Mark," she said. "It's Emily."

After that, she zoned out. His voice was distant and unimportant.

"Emily!"

She startled as her boss snapped her name down the phone.

"What? Sorry, I—I . . ."

"Did. You. Get. The damn cleaning contract or not?" He hurried the last few words. "Tell me they signed the contract. Emily?"

"Um—" She stuttered, trying to orientate her thoughts. "Contract?"

A hand reached over, and the middle-aged man took the phone from Emily. She couldn't have stopped him if she wanted to—her hand didn't have any grip, and she didn't have any grip on reality at the moment. She stared at the elderly faces looking down on her. She didn't recognize any. But why would she? She had never been here before. She then remembered why she was calling her boss.

"Cleaning contracts," she blurted out. "I sell cleaning contracts."

"That's right, love, but you're not selling anything today." The man gave a low laugh. "You just rest there. The ambulance is coming. I told your boss everything—he's worried about you."

"Mark, worried?" Emily laughed slightly too hard. Her head was sharp with pain, and she winced.

In the hospital, Emily lay very still, staring up at the cylindrical x-ray machine as it scanned her brain. It was making a sound—no, it was making sounds, plural. A voice over the intercom told her to keep still. She closed her eyes. Confined spaces frightened her; she had been given valium to calm her down, and she was now compliant and drowsy.

Some time passed, but Emily was not sure how long. She slept during the test results and then signed her name on the release papers: Emily Neville.

"Easy, Emily." Abbie helped Emily into her car.

After closing the passenger door, Emily watched her sister, whose long, blond hair blew effortlessly in the wind as she walked around the front of the car and got into the driver's side.

"Right, let's get you home," Abbie said.

Home? The word felt odd.

"Thanks for coming," Emily said.

"Of course. Just glad you're OK." Her sister's words sounded forced.

They pulled out of the hospital and onto the main road home. Emily wasn't sure why she had given the hospital her sister's number. The nurse had asked if she could call a family member, and she obliged by reciting her sister's number. Maybe the valium had impaired her memory. After all, it had been eight months since they had argued at their mum's funeral.

Emily must have dosed off again, because the next thing she knew, Abbie was at the passenger door helping her out.

She turned the key to her apartment and stepped inside. She didn't know why, but she half expected to see a staircase and wooden floors in front of her. But there were no stairs in her apartment.

"Are you OK, Emily?" Abbie looked genuinely concerned.

Emily tried a laugh. "Yeah—I'm fine."

"You look like shit, if you don't mind me saying so."

"I'm fine, Abigail. The CT scan showed nothing was wrong. It's the valium. I'll be right as rain tomorrow."

"All right, if you say so . . . Do you want me to stay?"

"No—thanks for coming, but I'll be fine."

"You're sure? I'll make you a coffee if you like."

Emily wanted to say no. She was still hurting, still mad at her big sister, but the word "OK" fell from her mouth instead.

Abbie smiled. "Great. You get into bed, and I'll bring it in."

She watched her sister scurry off into her kitchen.

On the way to her bedroom, Emily glanced into the living room. She saw the small red sofa she had bought from Ikea and the worn, discolored cream carpet her landlord had yet to replace. No steel mantel or fire. Emily sighed; there was a time she would have confided in Abbie, but those times had gone—Abbie's selfish actions had made sure of that. And anyway, if she didn't understand, how would anyone else? Just what had happened? A dream? If so, why would a dream still feel like actual past memories?

She changed and slipped into bed.

"Coffee, one sugar." Abbie set the drink on the bedside table. "Um, so I'll . . . I'll be off then!"

"Yeah . . . thanks," Emily said.

Abbie turned to the door. "See ya, then?"

Emily heard her sister's unspoken question but chose to ignore it. "Take care."

She soon heard the front door close and instantly felt guilty. It had been eight months; why was she still angry with Abbie? She fell back onto her pillow, and thoughts of the funeral filled her head. She had painful memories of walking behind the horse and cart that carried their mother, as per her funeral wishes. She walked shoulder to shoulder with her sister and stood next to her in the cathedral. It was a beautiful service.

Her thoughts drifted to the hours at the house after the service, when Abbie introduced Emily to Paul. That's when she had seen it—their mum's wedding ring on Abbie's ring finger. Abbie tried to explain that they had had to get married in secret since he was Iranian. Emily knew that, but why cut her out of the wedding? Emily didn't understand why Abbie kept it a secret from her. It was all too much to take in. Two months prior, they had found out their mum was dying, and now, her big sister was married—and with their mum's wedding ring! Was she not worthy of their mum's wedding ring? Why had Abbie not confided in her about the marriage? Was she not worthy of that either? Emily remembered screaming something about their dad and how he'd be turning in his grave, but that had been a step too far. All eyes had stared at her, dumbfounded, with open mouths and a deafening silence. Emily turned on her heels and ran out of their family home, never to go back.

That had been eight months ago, and she'd successfully avoided her sister's calls ever since. So why she'd given the nurse her number was somewhat baffling.

Emily woke early and took an Uber to the nursing home to collect her car. She also hoped she could set up a new meeting with the home manager so that come Monday, she could tell Mark she had another shot at the cleaning contract. It would also give her the perfect reason to be inside the nursing home, and she would need one if she wanted to find out why a knock to the head had made her dream about visiting her estranged sister Abigail—who was far from retirement home age—and who Valerie was. Had she really fabricated it all in her own mind? Emily thought not, and she had given this a lot of thought. She now recalled a time in high school when she had been running and fell. She was knocked unconscious but didn't have any kind of dream. Whenever she slept, she would always dream. But even her most real dream would feel like a dream once she woke, and something about this situation did not.

The night before, Emily's sleep had been broken, even with the valium still in her system. She couldn't stop thinking about the home—it had to mean something, she was sure of it. For the first part of her restless night, intrigue fueled her thoughts; however, as realization set in, fear took a strong hold in her mind. If this did mean something, if this home was alive in her subconscious, what did that mean for her grasp on reality?

She pushed open the door to the home, careful not to let it slam into the wall, and skulked up to the reception desk. Admittedly still a little embarrassed from her slip the day prior and nervous as to what this expedition would find, she waited. No one came.

Deciding this was the perfect time, Emily made her way into the communal area. The mismatching furniture was as it had been before; a few old folks were chatting and drinking tea, and it looked like a normal home. Briskly, she walked through to the elevators and pressed the button. The doors sprung open, and without hesitation, she entered. Emily's nerves rose with the elevator.

Once on the fourth floor, she walked slowly but deliberately along the dark corridor. The old paisley-patterned carpet stuck beneath her sneakers as she neared room 111. It all looked the same. She stared back down the corridor and then back at the white door, horrified by this realization. She had never physically been to the fourth floor—to any floor, for that matter. Anxiety boiled her blood, yet there was no blurred vision this time, and her limbs didn't feel heavy or light. She was sure this was real.

The door was real. Tiny fragments of a jaded experience tried to nuzzle into her mind. Had she really been thought this door before? Would she recognize the other side? Emily raised her fist and knocked hard. There was no answer. She knocked again and gave a few extra knuckle taps for good measure. Still no reply. She was moving her face toward the spy hole when she thought against getting too close to this increasingly mysterious door and took a step back. No one answered the door.

She retreated quickly back down the corridor the way she had come, each step raising her heartrate and questions about what had happened—no, what was still happening—to her. She should leave and never come back to this place. She had heard of all sorts of crazier things happening to people who knocked their heads. Some people were able to speak a whole new language. She just got a few days of random memories and somehow knew what the inside of a nursing home looked like, that's all.

Emily stopped dead, nearly falling over herself as she exited the elevator and started through the communal area. The room was now filled with elderly people. She rotated her head, watching old men and women chatting and others hobbling around. The noise was fairly loud for a nursing home, but then, it *was* Saturday. She edged through the room, wondering if they were really there or could see her. After all, her dream had felt real. Was she still dreaming? She contemplated making a run for it as thoughts of the walking dead started to unpick the fabric of her reality.

Emily relaxed when she saw the middle-aged man who had helped her; he was at reception. She was about to call out to him when a little voice stopped her.

"Ello," said the old, white-haired lady sitting by the window.

Emily approached warily, considering the fact that she had seen this woman in her . . . mind? "Hello."

The lady smiled up at Emily with a familiar warmth. Against all her better judgment, Emily felt at ease.

"Sit down, pet." The woman indicated the chair opposite her.

Emily sat. "The gardens are beautiful," she said politely, not knowing what else to say.

"As are you."

Emily smiled.

"Er, excuse me." She hesitated. "Can I ask you a question, please?" The lady nodded. "Do you know anyone called Valerie?"

"Why? Is she important to you?"

Emily didn't know how to answer that, but before she could speak, the old lady continued.

"People slip all the time, pet. You can help Valerie; she's on the other side. You can help yourself too."

Emily stood. "That's odd—that's a very strange thing to say." She stepped away.

"You asked."

Emily had now had just about had enough of this. "Look, I don't want to know about anything," she lied. She shook her head as if too free her thoughts. "Who is living in room 111?"

"Was."

"Was what?" Emily raised her voice. "Was what? Jesus Christ." The old lady nodded slowly. "OK. OK. Was what?" But the old lady didn't answer. "Was what?" Emily repeated, then panicked. The lady looked vacant. "Are you OK? Hello, lady? Are you all right?"

She looked toward the reception desk, saw the man who had helped her, and made a beeline for him.

He smiled warmly as she slammed into the desk.

"Nice to see you're OK," he said, not at all fazed by the manic behavior.

"I am, thanks. Look, I was just talking to that lady over there." She pointed at the white-haired lady. "And then she just zoned out on me—is she OK? She's not had a seizure or something, has she?" Emily breathed rapidly.

The man looked at the lady for a long moment. Emily wondered if she should repeat her question, but then he simply said, "Impossible."

She wondered why everything felt like one big riddle. "What's impossible?" She didn't try to hide her frustration. "I don't understand."

"Nor do I. That lady hasn't spoken since she arrived here." As if he registered her confusion, he carried on. "She came here six months ago from Sun

Life. Her family never visits, and we don't know her name because her paperwork somehow got lost."

Sun Life. Emily repeated the name in her head, recalling it from her vision. "Lost?" Emily said. "How can her information be lost?"

The man shrugged.

This was all getting to be a bit much for Emily. "OK, listen—can you tell me who is in room 111?"

"I'm not sure if I can do that."

"You can; look, my mum is going to live here." The words fell out without contemplation. "From Sun Life—I'm . . . I just want to know because . . . she said that she liked floor four when we visited." Emily smiled.

The man smiled.

Is he really buying this BS?

"She is," he said, and pointed to the white-haired lady. "She is in room 111."

Emily inhaled deeply. "No . . . I mean . . . I asked her, and she said . . ." *What did she say?* "Was! She said was."

The man eyed her suspiciously.

"OK. Listen, I'm going to level with you," she said, buying some time to think. "My mum . . . well, her room is next to a noisy resident in Sun Life, and I just want to be super sure before moving her here. Look. You look like a kind man; can you help me out? Put my mind at rest? Could you possibly tell me who *was* in room 111 before the white-haired lady?"

"They all have white hair here," he said under his breath and smiled.

Emily took the comment and ran with it. "I don't," she said, "and *if* I decide to move my mum here, I'll be your brown-haired lady." She smiled painfully; he had to be at least twenty years her senior.

But it did the trick, and the man tapped at the keyboard.

"Found it," he said.

Emily leaned forward to see.

"Like I said, another white-haired lady, called Valerie. She was actually lovely—she died six months ago. Sad, really—she always talked about her sister, but she never came to visit. I called her myself to arrange the funeral. Nice lady—Janice was her name. Only lives in the next town over, which I found odd. So close."

Emily felt the color drain from her face. She felt physically sick. Valerie was real?

"Are you OK?" the man asked.

"Yes," she lied.

Her world was literally changing in front of her, and no one else knew. She needed to get her feelings in check. She needed to find Valerie's sister Janice.

"You know what would make me feel sure that this home is the right place for my mum?" she said. "If I could talk to Janice. Could you write down her number for me?"

"Oh, I don't—"

"Please . . . I really want to be sure. And it would be so nice to see you each week when I come to visit."

The man hesitated

"Also, my company is bidding for the cleaning contract here, remember. It's not like I'm a complete stranger, is it? I just want to do my background research. And if I get the contract, we could do lunch together when I do site visits." Emily hoped his male instincts would cloud his judgment enough for her to get what she wanted.

And they did. "I'd like that," he said, writing out the number. "So do you want me to set you up a new meeting with the home manager?" He lowered his voice. "You didn't hear this from me, but the manager said she didn't like the guy from the other company. Offer a good price, and I know you'll get it." He winked and handed her the paper with the number written on.

She grabbed the number swiftly. "I'll swing by Monday when I have my schedule with me to get that set up—just came to pick up my car today, being the weekend and all." She edged toward the door. "Thanks for the number. Mum's the word," she said, placing a finger to her lips.

Emily hurried toward her car. *Well, winning that contract didn't go according to plan.* But at least she had a contact to Valerie.

*   *   *

Janice had been somewhat shocked when Emily called her house. She had been trying to get her grandchildren out the door in time for church. She agreed for Emily to come over that afternoon. Emily wasn't sure why Janice had agreed; she hadn't told her much over the phone, and what she *had* said must have sounded strange.

The night before, Emily had sat on her sofa staring down at the piece of paper with Janice's number written on it. She had stayed there all night, wondering how on earth she would explain. She had come to the somewhat sketchy conclusion that the memory of her talking to the photo must be a message or memory from Valerie to Janice. Emily obsessed over the new implanted memories she had. She thought of Valerie, the home itself, and why she was visiting her own sister. It had all felt so real. But it hadn't been real, it wasn't real—none of it was. She tried to close her eyes a few times to focus on the memories but quickly blinked them open. She wanted to see her home, to know she was still sitting on her own little red sofa. The nursing home plagued her thoughts most of the night. Emily was not unconscious when she spoke to the white-haired lady in the home, which would have been a comfort to Emily if not for the small fact that the woman didn't speak to anyone else.

By morning, Emily was dead set on wanting to move on with her life and forget about any knock to her head. But she knew that would never happen if she didn't speak with Valerie's sister, and though Emily wasn't sure about anything else, she was certain of that.

Emily sat in her car with the engine running. She stared at the cottage with its inconspicuous blue door and brown picket fence. It looked like any other country house, old and in need of repairs. She could see children's toys left behind by an excited child on the front lawn, and it reminded Emily of her own childhood home. She thought of her sister Abigail.

Switching off the ignition, Emily gingerly made for the house. She couldn't hear or see anyone inside. The sounds of children she had heard when she called earlier were gone, and it was now silent. But she knew Janice was in—she had told her to come at three p.m. sharp.

"Dear, don't be late," Janice had said. "I don't like people being late. And my husband will be here too," she had added.

Emily reached the door and took a moment to regroup her thoughts. She had expected Janice to cry when she phoned, but she didn't. The phone was silent, and Emily thought Janice had ended the call. Janice had then told Emily that Valerie hadn't made a will and that there was no money—her sister was not a wealthy person. Emily quickly insisted that she

was not some kind of weird scam artist; the thought
mortified her. She did her very best to convince Janice
that she honestly believed she had a message from her
sister. Janice was silent while Emily told her about the
photo of a woman standing next to a gorilla statue,
but after hearing that, she told Emily to come by
after church. Just like that.

So here she was. Emily pressed her finger into
the soft rubber button at the side of the door and
then waited for an answer. She wasn't waiting long
before she heard footsteps and a latch opening.
Emily stared at Janice for a while, motionless,
feeling as though she had seen a ghost. She had
prepared herself for this moment—after all, it was
the most obvious assumption. But now she was
there, standing in front of a complete stranger whom
she had already seen in her mind, and she felt giddy.
She swayed off balance, and the woman reached out
too steady her.

"I'm Janice," the old lady said, holding onto
Emily's elbow. "You must be Emily?"

Emily nodded.

Janice must have been at least fifteen or twenty
years older than the photo on the mantel, but she
was without doubt the same person. Emily stepped
through the door before stopping again.

"Are you OK, dear?" Janice was looking at Emily.

Emily swiveled her head around the entrance
hall. She felt her face flush hot. "No—no, I'm not. I

can't do this." She charged back out onto the front lawn, panting.

Emily sat on the doorstep next to Janice, clutching a cup of hot black coffee. She didn't care that it was slightly burning her hands; if it was hurting, then it was real. Part of her wanted to go inside to see the kitchen and the mantel holding the photo of Janice. But not yet.

Emily heard Janice whispering, telling her husband to go back upstairs. He had come out when Emily had run out onto the front lawn, and she wondered what he might think of her. A mad woman. And he'd be right. How on earth did she know what Janice's home looked like, and why?

"I'm going to level with you, Emily—I'm a bit confused by all this," Janice said eventually. "You recognized me and my entrance hall and think you know what my house looks like?" Emily nodded. "And that frightened you?" She nodded again. "And you talked to my dead sister—"

"I didn't know she was dead," Emily retorted. "I didn't know who you were till yesterday." Emily started to shake again.

"OK, dear." Janice patted Emily's knee. "Don't get worked up again."

Emily placed the cup on the ground and buried her face in her hands.

"Oh, come on now." Janice rubbed Emily's back.

Emily didn't ask her to stop. It felt nice, kind, and maternal.

Janice gave a little laugh, much like Valerie's. "I don't know what to say. It's all a bit odd, what you're saying."

"I don't know what I'm meant to do either." Emily looked up at Janice, her cheeks damp. "I feel like I'm meant to do something for her. Valerie, I mean."

Janice chucked. "Oh, Valerie could make most people feel like that. Even if they didn't want to. My little sister could wrap anyone around her little finger."

Emily smiled up at her. "You have the same laugh."

"That's right," Janice said simply. "Look, we can't sit out here all afternoon—my neighbors will start to gossip. Let's go inside. It's OK. You'll be all right."

Inside, Emily touched the banister, looking up at the stairs she remembered climbing to bed. However, she had no memory of the bedroom. The wooden floor tapped under her shoes.

"There's a key hook on the wall behind the kitchen door?" Emily said.

Janice nodded in agreement.

"The living room. Can I see your—" Emily stopped. "Sorry." She grimaced. "I must sound crazy."

"A little." Janice laughed and led her into the living room. She looked at Emily. "Do you recognize it?"

"Yes," Emily said, looking at the worn brown leather sofa. "But it was nighttime in my memory, vision, whatever it was." Emily walked over to the mantel, stepping around the white rug to pick up the framed photo.

"That's why I let you come—when you mentioned the photo," Janice said.

Emily glanced at Janice and then back at the picture. "Did she take this—Valerie? Did Valerie take this of you?"

Janice joined Emily and took the picture out of her hand. "No," she said, and started to undo the back of the frame. "My son did."

Emily watched Janice unfold half of the photograph and hand it back to her. To the far right stood Valerie, laughing and covering her mouth with her hand. She looked younger—they both did. And happy—so what changed?

Then she noticed a gem on Valerie's hand. "The ring." Emily pointed. "Her ring." She looked at Janice. "She takes it off to—"

"Clean," Janice finished. "That's right. But that's our nan's ring. Valerie took it when she died. Our nan would always take it off to clean." Janice laughed at the memory. "Nanna Abigail. She was always rummaging around in the apron for that damn ring."

"Abigail," said Emily. "That's my sister's name. So what happened between you? You look so happy in the photo."

Janice turned to sit on the sofa, explaining her knees were not what they used to be. Emily followed, picture in hand. They sat for a while, not speaking. Emily didn't feel it was her place to fire more questions at Janice. She had been kind enough to entertain this ludicrous notion, and Emily wasn't about to push the envelope.

A few more seconds passed, and Janice reached for the photo, taking it from Emily's hand.

She said, "You said that Valerie told you that—"

Emily stopped her. "Valerie never told me anything. I just know. It's like I knew the words to say, but not the actual event. Wow, I sound insane—I *feel* insane," she added honestly. "The memories I was telling the photo about. I was standing right there." She pointed to the mantel. "And I was talking to the person in the photo—you, but I didn't know that then." She paused, trying to find the right words to explain. "I don't actually have a memory of what I was saying. Does that make sense? Even a little?"

Janice didn't answer, so Emily continued. "OK, so I remember telling the photo about a square building, and the windows were too high to see out of. But I don't actually have a physical memory of this building or the windows—it was as if Valerie had told me, but I don't remember her telling me. I just remember telling the photo." Emily tried to get a gauge of Janice's thoughts; had this gone too far?

Janice stood and walked out the room.

Well, that's odd. But then, Emily's whole life was feeling odd right now. She wondered if Janice had gone to call the police and if she was in the kitchen asking them to bring a doctor with a straightjacket. Should she be worried?

"Red wine," Janice said, walking back into the living room and handing a glass to Emily.

Emily was standing by the window. She had been wondering if Janice's sudden exit was her cue to leave. "Thank you." She hesitantly took the glass. It clearly wasn't time to leave, so she followed Janice back to the sofa.

"I like a red, even at my age," Janice said. "So did Valerie." Her tone was even.

The mood had shifted, and Emily wasn't quite sure how to respond. She sat next to Janice, keeping one eye on the door. She wasn't sure who was acting crazier now—her or Janice.

"OK, Emily, tell me everything you said to the photo."

Emily finished telling her about the building with the high windows.

"It was 1949," Janice said. "The building you spokeof—it was a hospital, a quarantine facility."

"Quarantine?" Emily echoed.

"Valerie was four. She contracted scarlet fever, and in those days, you were quarantined for that. It was serious. I can remember walking there, to the hospital, with our mum. They let us pick up her clothes to wash and bring fresh ones back, but we couldn't see her. The building had high windows. I remember thinking they were so high that not even grown-ups could see in or out. She was there for a month."

Emily recoiled backward. "A month? And you couldn't see her?" Emily couldn't hold back the disbelief in her question. "But she was only four. Just a baby."

"Yes, I know. But that's how it was. I can only imagine how scared she must have felt, abandoned." There was a pause, and Janice said, "We never spoke about it."

Emily was confused. "Spoke about what?"

"About any of it. She came home, and that was that."

"Didn't you tell her you weren't allowed to see her, though?"

Janice gave a fake, slightly-patronizing laugh. "Haha, I'm sure Mum told her, and the doctors, but she was four. So even if they had explained, it wouldn't have made a difference. We left her there, and that was that in her eyes."

Emily didn't have anything to say, and Janice sat in silence for a while.

Janice finally spoke. "I never thought she would remember that much about it, or that it had upset her so much. If I had known—" She stopped and gave Emily a warm, genuine smile, not dissimilar to the same warm smile Emily had seen on Valerie's face in the nursing home. "I wished I'd spoken to her more, but I wasn't that type. I didn't know how to do deep and meaningful the way you youngsters do now. Brush it under the rug—that was how I dealt with things. I didn't know it would affect her."

"Well, of course it would; she was left in quarantine for a month. How would *you* like it?" Emily blurted out. She instantly felt remorseful as she saw the pain on Janice's face. "Sorry."

Janice simply replied, "It was a different time back then."

Emily hung her head. She took a sip of wine to distract from the awkwardness her comments had caused. It was dry, leaving a film on the roof of her mouth. She placed it on a small coffee table.

"Not a wine drinker?"

"Sorry. No."

Janice nodded. "I have white if you prefer."

"I'm good, thanks. I don't drink much wine, if I'm honest." She didn't want to dwell on yet another odd revelation. "Tell me more—I want to know more."

"When we were young, our father was at war, so my mum was running the house while working.

Our Nanna Abigail looked after Valerie, what with her being so young. I was that much older, so I helped Mum. I remember Valerie taking it hard when Nanna died—we all did, but her more so. Nanna practically raised her."

"I don't remember anything about her in my dream—vision. God, I have no idea what to call it."

They both laughed at how surreal the situation felt.

"Well, that was one time when we *did* cry. Maybe we should have shown our emotions more. Presumably, she felt at peace with it."

Emily shrugged. "Maybe."

"What else did you tell my picture?" Janice asked, and Emily told her.

Janice slid back onto the sofa for a more comfortable position. "Yes, I remember the airport. I was scared myself, and I didn't want to tell her not to go, but like I said, it was different back then. Meaningful conversation felt awkward to me, you know? No, you probably don't."

Emily lowered her head. "I do, actually. I'm not the best at expressing myself either. I just get angry and don't listen."

Janice gave a knowing look and continued. "She met Jack, and before we knew it, she was moving to Texas, just like that."

A noise from the hallway indicated that Janice's husband was bored of skulking upstairs. Footsteps came from the kitchen, and Janice smiled as if to put Emily at ease.

"Maybe I should have told her not to go," Janice went on. "I didn't think it would make any difference what I thought. I missed her so badly when she went, and I worried for my little sister."

"Didn't you want to visit her?"

Janice nodded. "I had my own family by then and had never been on a plane. Still haven't."

"What? Seriously? You've never flown?"

"Nope. Bob has." Emily presumed Bob was Janice's husband.

"Right."

Janice went on. "Then they broke up, Jack and Valerie. Our mum and dad flew out to see her, and I half expected her to come back with them, but she didn't." There was a long pause. "I didn't realize she wanted me to tell her to come home. She stopped calling, and I stopped calling her. Then she met Chuck." Janice looked over at the photo in Emily's hand. "But Valerie told you she was happy? That's good to know."

"Yes, she was happy with Chuck . . . So, the photo? When was that taken?" Emily asked.

"She came to England with Chuck, something to do with his work. They flew in for a week and were off again. Only spent a day with us—half a day, really. The rest of the time, she traveled the country seeing old friends. We had a picnic in Crystal Palace Park in south London," Janice explained. "That's when the picture was taken—by the gorilla statue, by the big lake there. It was lovely, but I was hurt that she didn't want to spend more time with me. When she left, I got so upset with her over it I never called her again. My son put the picture on the mantel, and I folded her out of sight."

"That's so sad," Emily said. "All these years, and it sounds like you could have sorted it out with a few heartfelt conversations."

There was a pause before Janice said, "Looks that way, doesn't it?"

"You live so close to the home; why didn't you visit?"

"I didn't know she was there. Last I heard, Chuck had died, and she was still living in Texas. I couldn't believe it when I got the call from the home."

"But she gave the home your number for an emergency contact?"

Janice looked deflated. "I know—I don't know why she didn't call me. Stubborn, I suppose. She wasn't even that old. Seventy-two."

Emily did the math; Janice was seventy-six.

"An aneurism, apparently," Janice continued. "Makes you think, doesn't it? Life is short, time got away from us."

They sat in silence. Emily's thoughts now drifted away from Valerie and toward her own sister, Abbie.

She checked her watch. It was getting late.

"I, er . . ."

"I know; it's late." Janice stood.

Emily walked to the door. "I don't really know why all this happened. But I hope it helps in some way, Janice. If you ask me, Valerie didn't want to rest until she had made her peace with you. Talk to her. She is clearly here with you. I mean, if she wasn't, how else would I have known what your house looked like?"

"That's because this was the house we grew up in." Janice smiled knowingly.

"But you didn't have that expensive white rug in the 50s or the photo on the mantel, did you?" Emily saw the realization on Janice's face. "Talk to her."

Janice smiled. "Thank you. You've just given two old women a restful life, past and present. I think you might have a gift, dear." She closed the door.

Emily slid into her car, knowing that an odd but amazing thing had just happened. So why didn't she feel as complete as Janice appeared?

Were Emily and Abigail on the same course as Valerie and Janice? Was that what this was all about? Did Valerie want to use Emily to reconcile with her sister, and in return give her a gift? A gift of peace, to let go of the hurt and misunderstanding? Emily's heart spontaneously started to beat faster at the realization. A few heartfelt conversations could have fixed Valerie and Janice, and it could also fix her and Abigail—if she would let it. Emily shuddered.

Valerie was living so close to Janice and was too stubborn to contact her, and then an aneurism ended all chances.

Was she Valerie? Would she be the one living in some home, probably Sun Life, bitter that Abbie never told her about the wedding, about the ring? And was it really worth falling out over? After all, she had never listened to Abbie's reasons why, and *someone* had to get their mum's wedding ring. A sinking feeling grounded her. What had she done?

"Oh god, Abigail," Emily said out loud and reached for her phone. She dialed the number.

"Hello?"

From the Author

Thank you for reading Slip. If you enjoyed it, I would be grateful for a review. A review is the best gift you could give an author as it helps the books visibility for other potential readers. You can leave a review at Amazon or the online retailers where you bought the book, and on GoodReads. com. Feel free to leave a short sentence, or longer. Every little helps.

Slip, the back story—
Visit VixBrowneAuthor.com/blog and search Slip.

COMING SOON 2019
'*Now & Then*'
A Novel

VixBrowneAuthor.com

www.ingramcontent.com/pod-product-compliance
Lightning Source LLC
Chambersburg PA
CBHW050914120626
46552CB00004B/1559